Pete the Cat

Big Easter Adventure

by
Kimberly
and
James Dean

HARPER

An Imprint of HarperCollinsPublishers

Harperfestival is an imprint of HarperCollins Publishers.
Copyright © by James Dean (for the character of Pete the Cat)
Pete the Cat: Big Easter Adventure
Copyright © 2014 by James Dean. All rights reserved.
Manufactured in China.

Library of Congress catalog card number: 2013944039
ISBN 978-0-06-219867-9
13 14 15 16 17   SCP   10 9 8 7 6 5 4 3 2 1

First Edition

Pete was excited! Easter was here! He couldn't wait for his basket of goodies. Jelly beans were his favorite.

Pete put on the bunny ears and thought, A cat
with ears like a bunny—now that's funny!

"Happy Easter, chickens! Do you have any eggs today?" Pete asked. "I am helping the Easter Bunny."

"Sure, Pete. We have a lot of eggs," the chickens said. "We are happy to help, but don't you need a bunny nose and fluffy bunny tail?"

The chickens were right. A bunny nose and tail
would be neat. Then Pete's costume would be complete!

Pete put on the nose
and tail like a bunny's.
A cat dressed up like
a bunny—
now that's funny!

Now Pete was ready. It was getting late,
and he still had a lot of eggs to decorate!
What colors would Pete use?

Hop! Hop! Hop!

Off to the toolshed for paint and brushes.

Some eggs had one color.
Some eggs had two.
Some eggs were red,
and some eggs were blue!

When the egg-painting was done, Pete had
a basket full of bright, colorful, amazing eggs!
Now hiding them would be lots of fun.

But where, oh where, would Pete hide the eggs?

Around the neighborhood—for all his friends to find!

Pete hid eggs in flower pots.
He hid them in the water spout.
And when he was done hiding the eggs,
Pete the Cat was all worn out!

"Helping others out
is what Easter is all about,"
Pete said.

Pete's job was done. He was hiding the last one . . . when the Easter Bunny arrived.

"Great job, Pete! You were a big help," said the Easter Bunny.

The Easter Bunny
gave Pete an award
for a job well done.

Helping others can be lots of fun!

HAPPY EASTER, EVERYBODY!